IGGY THE URK:

FoL

Please return on or before the latest date above.
You can renew online at *www.kent.gov.uk/libs*
or by telephone 08458 247 200

Libraries & Archives

Kent
County
Council

00884\DTP\RN\07.07   LIB 7

IGGY THE URK: BOOOM!

Alan MacDonald

Illustrated by Mark Beech

First published in 2011
by Bloomsbury Publishing plc
This Large Print edition published by
AudioGO Ltd 2012
by arrangement with
Bloomsbury Publishing plc

ISBN: 978 1445 823577

British Library Cataloguing in Publication Data available

Printed and bound in Great Britain by
MPG Books Group Limited

Contents

Long, long ago...

Really ages ago. The world was a wild and barren place. There were no houses or shops, no schools or teachers, no cars, flushing toilets or peanut-butter sandwiches. So many things didn't exist that to write them all down would fill every page of this book and leave no room for the story.

If you want to imagine how the world was, imagine an endless landscape of mountains, forests, rocks and stones. In fact, stones lay everywhere, because this was . . .

THE STONE AGE

In the forests lived savage beasts—bears, snaggle-toothed tigers and woolly mammoths, which looked like elephants badly in need of a haircut. People generally avoided the forests. They lived together in tribes because it was safer that way and easier on the cooking. One such tribe was the Urks.

The Urks were a warlike race with bushy beards and hairy legs—especially some of the women. Their clothes were made of animal skins and they lived in caves high on a hill, overlooking the Valley of Urk and the river winding through it. In one of these caves lived a boy called Iggy. He wasn't the tallest or the hairiest in his tribe, but what he

2

did have was imagination, and this got him into a whole heap of trouble. That of course is another story . . . Luckily it's the story that's about to begin . . .

did have was imagination, and this got
him into a whole heap of trouble. That
of course is unfortunately . . . Luckily
it's the story that's about to begin . . .

Chapter 1
Making a Splash

It had been raining solidly in the Valley
of Urk for three days. Rain dripped
from trees and noses and trickled down
necks. The rain turned the hillside to
mud and pattered in puddles the size
of small lakes. The older Urks nodded
their heads wisely and said it was the
start of the rainy season (which came
after the foggy season and before the

cold season).

Iggy was fed up with sitting in his cave, listening to the plip-plop of the rain and trying to keep the fire from going out. For the hundredth time he stood at the entrance peering through the steady drizzle. The dark clouds over the mountains were beginning to roll away at last leaving a bright patch of blue sky. In the valley below, the River Urk had risen high. To Iggy that meant one thing: swimming at Giant's Rock.

*   *   *

An hour later he said goodbye to his mum and set off down the hill, calling for his best friend, Hubba, on the way. Giant's Rock was a little way downstream. It overlooked a bend in the river where the rocks cast long shadows over a deep pool. When they arrived there were already half a dozen Sons of Urk splashing and laughing in the shallows. Iggy waded into the cool green water to join them.

'Hey! Watch this!'

Iggy looked up. Someone was perched on the very top of Giant's Rock, preparing to dive. It could only be Snark. Jumping off the rocks was a game the young Urks often played, daring each other to go higher and higher, but as usual Snark was showing off by choosing the highest rock of all. Giant's Rock was so tall, just looking up at it made Iggy feel dizzy.

Snark waved at them, satisfied he'd got the attention of his audience now. Backing up, he took a short run, raised his arms and sprang nimbly from the rock. He swooped down, spinning into a double corkscrew before entering the water as cleanly as a salmon. For a few seconds there was nothing to be seen but a circle of ripples, then Snark burst to the surface. He wiped his eyes and shook his head, spraying Iggy like a wet dog.

'WOOO!' he whooped. 'See that?'

'Brilliant!' 'Deadly!' chorused the other Urks.

Snark raised a hand to acknowledge their applause. He knew very well he was probably the best swimmer in the tribe—which wasn't saying much since most Urks couldn't swim at all. He smoothed back his glossy hair and went to sit on a rock.

'Who's next then?' he asked.

Iggy groaned inwardly. Why did everything with Snark have to be a competition?

'What about you, pig-breath?' said Snark, turning on Iggy.

'Me? I've done it before. Loads of times,' said Iggy.

'Yeah? When?'

'You know. That um . . . time when it rained. Remember, Hubba? We both did.' Iggy nodded meaningfully at his friend, hoping he would back him up.

Hubba frowned. '*Did* we? I don't remember.'

Snark folded his arms. 'Well, here's your chance, dung-brain. Show us.'

'What—now?' Iggy looked up at the towering brown rock. 'Like you said, you done it loads of times. It's easy. 'Less of course you're scared.'

'Scared?'

'Go on, Iggy,' said Hubba. 'Show 'em.'

*   *   *

Ten minutes later Iggy stood on top of Giant's Rock, his head almost level with the tops of the trees. In the distance the grey mountains rose up with the craggy peak of Old Grumbly hidden in the clouds. Across the river the forest stretched away as far as the eye could see. On a clear day it was a glorious view—if you weren't about to jump to your death. Iggy edged forward a few faltering steps

8

and leaned out. The river below was a sickeningly long way down. He could see the others looking up at him, waiting to see if he would lose his nerve. He inched forward a little more, his legs starting to tremble.

'JUMP!' Snark's shout echoed off the rocks.

'You can do it, Iggy!' shouted Hubba.

Easy for you to say, thought Iggy. *You're not standing where I am.* His palms were sticky with sweat and his heart beat madly like a drum. The green pool below didn't look much to aim at. What if he didn't jump out far enough and bounced off the jagged rocks? What if he forgot to hold his breath when he hit the water? He should never have let Snark talk him into this.

'Get on with it! JUMP!' yelled Snark.

The others began to chant, their voices growing louder and faster.

'JUMP!JUMP!JUMP!JUMP!'

Iggy knew it was now or never. He closed his eyes and tried not to think about the drop or the rocks or the possibility of drowning. Blowing out his cheeks, he ran at the edge. At the last

9

moment he made the mistake of opening his eyes and looking down. Help! For a moment he tottered on the edge, one foot in mid-air and the other on the rock, his arms whirling furiously. Then . . .

'WAAAARGHHHHHHHHHHHH!'

SPLASH!

Everything went dark green. Iggy glimpsed bubbles, clouds of weed and people's legs—which looked funny underwater. Then his head broke the surface and he was gasping for breath.

Snark was doubled up laughing.

'HA HA! That were so funny! Your face!'

Iggy ignored him. He swam a few ungainly strokes towards the bank, then waded the rest of the way before flopping down on the grass. He caught sight of some of the younger Urks doing impressions of how he hit the water—like a two-ton mammoth doing a bellyflop. No doubt Snark would enjoy telling the story around the fire tonight. Iggy lay down, dripping wet, waiting to get his breath back. At least he hadn't chickened out in front of everyone. It was funny, he thought, the way you sort of shot back to the surface. Hubba joined him on the bank.

'Great bellyflop,' he said. 'Deadly.'

'Thanks.'

They were silent for a while, watching the river drift by.

'Hubba, you ever wondered why things float?' asked Iggy.

Hubba wrinkled his nose. 'Nope.'

'We float. And fishes—you never see a fish sink.'

'S'pose not.'

'But why not?' said Iggy. He picked up a small rock and tossed it into the river. It vanished with a loud *plop*!

'See? A rock sinks.'

'Can't swim,' grunted Hubba. 'Rocks never learned.'

Iggy shook his head. 'It's nothing to do with swimming. Some things float and some don't. There must be a reason.'

Hubba shrugged and lay down. Thinking always gave him a headache. But Iggy went on gazing at the river, making a list in his head.

Wouldn't it be something, thought Iggy, *if you could float downriver on a leaf?*

11

Obviously a leaf couldn't carry you, but a log would. Logs floated—as Iggy had once discovered when he was escaping from a tribe of angry Nonecks. But a log wasn't safe. You had to hold on for dear life while it bobbed and rolled and threatened to tip you off. What he needed was something you could sit in—or on. A floater or boater or something. He shivered. Looking up, he saw someone standing over him casting a dark shadow. Snark. Why couldn't the big blathermouth leave him alone? Iggy had never noticed before how thick and hairy his legs were—much like his head.

'Not drowned then?' said Snark. 'Pity.'

Snark plonked himself down beside Iggy, uninvited. Evidently he had something on his mind.

'I hear he's making his mind up,' he said. 'At long last.'

'Who?' said Iggy.

'Hammerhead, of course. Hasn't you heard? He's choosing the next Chief tonight—at the Naming Ceremony.'

Iggy sat up. This was news to him. He knew that his Uncle Ham had been grumbling lately that he was getting too old to be Chief, but he was always grumbling about something. Iggy had no idea he was actually thinking of naming his successor. He had heard his dad talk about the Naming Ceremony. The only time it happened was when a chief had no obvious successor. Hammerhead had only one daughter, Umily, and no sons, so no one was certain what would happen when he died and went to join the Ancestors. Some claimed Iggy's dad (as Hammerhead's brother) would become Chief, while others put forward various other names. Either way, it was for Hammerhead to decide by means of the ancient Naming Ceremony.

'So who you reckon it'll be?' asked Snark.

'I don't know,' said Iggy. 'What about Umily?'

Snark snorted. 'HER? She's a girl!'

'But still, she's a Chief's daughter.'

'No,' said Snark, dismissing the idea. 'It's got to be someone strong. Clever. Hairy. A proper Chief.'

'Like who?' said Hubba. Snark leaned forward.

14

'Like my dad.'

'*Borg*?' Hubba laughed out loud. 'You think Hammerhead's gonna choose *him*?'

'Oh he will, you'll see,' said Snark sourly. 'When the Chief's gone, my dad takes over, mark my words. And when he does, I'd watch out if I was you.'

He gave them a dark look and strode off, collecting his spear from the rocks. Hubba watched him climb the hill. 'Slugface,' he remarked.

'Don't listen to 'im, Iggy.'

'Don't worry,' said Iggy. All the same he felt a little uneasy about the Naming Ceremony. He hoped that Hammerhead knew what he was doing.

Chapter 2
Dribble Dobble, Dib Dab

It looked like the whole tribe had turned out for the Naming Ceremony. Most of them had never attended one before, as Hammerhead had been Chief for what seemed like for ever. As darkness fell, they gathered by the Standing Stone. A crackling fire lit the filthy, hairy faces on the front row, where many of the women had taken their place. Everyone was eager to find out who would be chosen as the next High Chief, the one who would eventually step into Hammerhead's shoes (at least if he'd had any shoes).

Iggy looked round the ragged circle, wondering which of them would be chosen. The six wrinkled elders were there, although Sedric had already dozed off, as usual. Iggy's dad sat on the Chief's left, wearing a worried expression. Hammerhead stepped into the firelight and raised his hand to command silence.

'Friends, brothers, sisters, Urks,' he said, hoping that covered just about everyone. 'As you know, I has been your Chief for a good many years. Some might say I been a good Chief, perhaps even a great one . . .' He paused in case anyone wanted to cheer—they didn't. 'But no Chief lives for ever, not even me. The day will come when I can't . . . um . . . do the things a Chief does.'

The Urks looked blank. As far as they could tell a Chief slept till noon and helped himself to gigantic helpings of roast meat. It didn't exactly seem like a heavy burden.

Hammerhead pressed on regardless. 'That is why I has decided to name the Chief who'll come after me. One of you must lead the tribe of Urk into the new dawn.'

Across the circle, Iggy caught sight of Snark wearing a confident smirk. Iggy remembered what he'd said by the river. If Borg, his father, ever became Chief they had better watch their backs.

Iggy had wondered if the ceremony would include some trial of strength or hunting skills, but it turned out the Chief would be chosen in the traditional Urk way—with the aid of a blindfold and a pointy stick. Hammerhead had the stick in his hand now and was dipping it into a bowl of red gunk that looked like the innards of a pig. He held up the stick  for everyone to see, dripping sticky red globs into the dust.

'Whoever is marked with the blood, he shall be Chief!' he declared. Borg came forward to blindfold him with a strip of hide. When it was done he held up three fingers in front of the Chief's face.

'How many fingers does you see?'

'Twelve!' said Hammerhead, taking a wild guess. Borg nodded, satisfied that everything was in order. He stood behind the Chief to tighten the blindfold one last time.

'Choose wisely,' he whispered in his ear. 'Listen for my cough.'

'Your cloth?' said Hammerhead.

'My *cough*, you deaf clod!' hissed Borg. 'I'll cough twice. Don't forget.'

He gripped Hammerhead by the shoulders and spun him round three times so that there could be no accusations of cheating. Borg then retired to take his place in the circle, leaving Hammerhead alone in the middle clutching his sticky stick. All that spinning round had made the Chief dizzy and he staggered to one side. Somewhere behind him the fire crackled and he made a mental note not to burn his bottom like the last time he was blindfolded.

Standing in the circle, Iggy watched as the Chief took a few unsteady steps forward. He waggled the stick in front of him and spoke the words of the ancient ceremony:

Ip dip my little stick,
Dribble dobble, dib dab,
Which one's IT?

The Chief kept walking, heading straight for a young Urk called Pud, who was nobody's idea of a future Chief. Someone in the circle coughed loudly. Hammerhead seemed to hear it because he suddenly changed direction, lurching to his right. He took three or four paces and stopped—right in front of Snark's father. Iggy held his breath. Surely he wasn't going to choose Borg of all people—Borg, who regarded Hammerhead and everyone else as blundering idiots? Borg, who had once left a deadly black scorpion in the Chief's cave claiming he thought it was a crab?

Iggy could hardly bear to watch as the dripping stick reached out just short of Borg's forehead and paused. Very slowly, so as not to make it obvious, Borg began to lean forward to meet it. All his life

21

he had waited for this moment and now finally it had arrived. He coughed again. Suddenly the stick jerked away and Hammerhead was off, wandering around blindly again. Halfway round the circle he stopped as if obeying some inner voice. Iggy watched in alarm as he took three paces forward. He was heading straight towards . . . argh! Towards *him*! The blobby stick reached out . . . 'OUCH!' said Iggy as it poked him in the nose, leaving a sticky red mark.

'The Spirits have chosen!' cried Gaga the Wise. Hammerhead pulled off his blindfold.

'IGGY!' he beamed, clasping him in a bear hug.

'*Iggy?*' chorused several voices.

'*Iggy?*' seethed Borg, crimson with rage.

Iggy looked at the faces in the circle, all staring at him in bug-eyed disbelief.

'Um . . . best of three?' he said.

*   *   *

Back in his cave, Borg stamped up and down, kicking a bone out of his way. He

22

wasn't a patient man, as everyone knew, but this time Hammerhead had pushed him too far.

'Iggy?' he fumed. 'That runty little scroggler? It's his nephew, for the love of Urk!'

Snark sighed. 'It were just bad luck!'

'Luck my eye!' thundered Borg. 'Hammerhead did this on purpose. He cheated!'

'You wanted him to cheat,' Snark pointed out.

'Of course I did. He were meant to pick me! I explained it to him clear as mud. But the fathead walked right past me.'

'Maybe he didn't see you,' suggested Snark.

'He were wearing a blindfold, dung brain. How could he see me?'

Snark shrugged. 'I don't know. How come he seen Iggy? How did he cheat?'

Borg growled and turned away. All he knew was that he had been robbed—robbed by a skinny little brat who shouldn't be in charge of an ants' nest. For years he had slaved for this, plotted and schemed to become Chief—and

23

now, just when the prize was in his grasp, it had been snatched away by a low-down, filthy trick. The worst of it all was Iggy was still a boy—he might be Chief for years. No, Borg decided—Hammerhead wouldn't get away with this. He would pay.

'There's only one thing for it,' he said. 'We has to get rid of them.'

'You mean kill 'em?' said Snark hopefully. 'Iggy too?'

''Course him too. The question is how? It has to be done clever and quiet. No one must suspect.'

'I could drop a boulder on Iggy's head,' suggested Snark.

'I said "clever",' sighed Borg.

'Two boulders? One for Hammerhead.'

Borg rolled his eyes. 'If we kill 'em both at once it'll look too obvious. People will start asking questions. Unless . . .' Borg stopped pacing the cave. An evil light entered his eyes.

'Unless what?' said Snark.

'We get someone else to do it.'

Snark looked puzzled. 'Who?'

'Remember that tribe,' said Borg, 'the one that attacked us last winter?'

24

Snark turned pale. 'You mean Nonecks? But they're savages.'

'Exactly,' nodded Borg. 'That's why we're going to pay them a visit.'

Chapter 3

Floaters and Sinkers

The next morning Iggy went in search of Hubba. Usually he turned up at Iggy's cave the moment he saw the smoke from a fire, but today Iggy found him down the hill, sorting through his rock collection. Hubba collected rocks for the simple reason that they were easy to find—the hillside was littered with them. Feathers or shells might have been more interesting but they were a lot more effort. Iggy hadn't had much chance to speak to his friend since the Naming Ceremony and there was something he wanted to show him.

'Hey, Hubba—come to the river,' he said.

Hubba didn't look up. 'Can't. I'm busy.'

'It's a surprise. Come and see!'

Normally Hubba couldn't resist a surprise but this time he gave a weary shrug. 'Thought you'd be busy,' he said.

'Busy?'

'You being High Chief an' all. I expect you got big important stuff to do.'

Iggy stared at him. 'What are you on about? It's me—Iggy!'

'I can see that. I aren't stupid,' said Hubba sulkily.

'And I'm not Chief yet—Hammerhead could go on for years,' Iggy pointed out. 'Anyway, it wasn't my idea. I didn't ask to be chosen.'

Hubba went on sorting rocks into different colours: grey, light grey, dark grey . . .

'Still, it's different now, isn't it?' he mumbled.

'Why?'

'Like I said, you got meetings with elders and that. You don't want to waste time messin' around with me.'

Iggy crouched down beside him. 'Of course I do, you noggerhead! You're my best friend.'

Hubba squinted at him. 'Who you calling noggerhead?'

'You, noggerhead!' Iggy pushed him over. 'Come on, I'll race you to the river!'

They chased down the hill. Iggy arrived first, though Hubba claimed that he had a head start.

'So where is it?' asked Hubba, panting for breath. 'The big surprise?'

'Wait there—I'll show you,' said Iggy. He went haring off along the bank and disappeared through the trees. For a while Hubba heard nothing, then there was a loud splash as something hit the water. A moment later Iggy came into view, up to his waist in the river and pulling a strange-looking thing behind him. It was made out of woven twigs and bobbed along like a giant bird's nest.

Hubba knitted his brows. 'What is it?'

'A boater. What do you think?'

'Yeah—deadly,' said Hubba uncertainly.

'It's made of twigs, leaves and mud. You know why?'

'You run out of rocks?' said Hubba.

'No. They're all things that float—apart from mud, of course, but that's holding it together.'

'So how's it catch 'em exactly?' asked Hubba.

'What?'

'The fishes.'

'It's not for fishing. It's a boater,' said Iggy. 'You sit inside here and it carries you along the river.'

'Ah. Right. Why?'

'Because that's the idea—you float.'

Hubba doubted this, but he didn't want to sound critical. Most of Iggy's ideas sounded crackpot at first—and one or two of them even worked.

'Show us then,' he said.

'All right,' said Iggy. 'Come on—we'll go for a trip.'

Hubba gaped at him. 'What? In that?'

'It's quite safe. See, it floats!'

Hubba sighed heavily. He knew he was going to regret this.

Getting into the boater proved harder than Iggy expected. It spun round, wobbling and bobbing away as if it was playing a game with them. Eventually Iggy managed to climb on board, but when Hubba tried to join him the boater tipped up alarmingly and water sloshed inside. There wasn't a lot of room to get comfortable, but at last they got their legs untangled and were ready to set off.

'Now what?' asked Hubba, clinging to the sides.

'Nothing. We sit back and the current takes us.'

Hubba looked blank.

'The current,' said Iggy. 'The river sort of wibbles in one direction—haven't you noticed?'

Hubba couldn't say he had. You could paddle in water, or even swim in it if you really had to, but it wasn't meant for bobbing and wibbling. His feet were cold already, not to mention his bottom. He shifted in his seat.

'Iggy, it's wet in here.'

'Stop worrying. Enjoy it!' said Iggy. 'Look, we're coming to Giant's Rock!'

Hubba looked towards the bank,

wishing that he had never left it. Despite spinning in circles they had drifted some way downstream where the river was deeper and the current stronger.

'I'm wet!' he grumbled. 'My bottom's leaking!'

'Stop moaning!' said Iggy, who was trying, without much success, to steer.

Hubba stood up suddenly, rocking them dangerously. 'We're sinking!' he yelped.

'Sit down. You'll tip us over!'

'But we are! Look!'

Iggy looked down at his feet. He was shocked to see how much dirty water had got into the boater. It sloshed around his ankles. It seemed to be trickling in through the tiny gaps between the woven

31

twigs where the mud was—or used to be.

'Quick,' he cried. 'Get it out!' He knelt down, scooping up water in an attempt to bail it out. Hubba tried to help, but that made the boater rock more wildly. As fast as they threw water out, more seeped back in to take its place. They were sinking lower.

'Do something, Iggy!' wailed Hubba.

'What?'

Hubba suddenly had an idea. The water was coming in so it followed they had to let it out—and quickly. There was one easy way to do that. Hubba raised his foot.

'NO!' cried Iggy. But he was too late, Hubba brought his heel down hard in the bottom of the boat.

A gaping hole appeared, and water immediately rushed in instead of going out as Hubba had expected. The boater went down with a final gloop and glug, taking its crew with it.

For a few seconds Iggy tried to hang on, but it was no use. The two of them thrashed around in the river, struggling towards the bank with ungainly strokes. Neither of them were strong swimmers, but luckily they didn't have far to go before their feet touched squelchy mud.

Iggy stood up, coughing and dripping. It was a few moments before he noticed someone perched on a rock, grinning at him. It was Umily. *Perfect*, thought Iggy—*she must have seen the whole disaster from start to finish.*

'How's the water?' she asked.

'Yeah, very funny,' replied Iggy, squelching on to the bank.

'So what was you trying to do? I'm just interested.'

Iggy sighed, not in the mood for long explanations. 'It's a boater,' he said. 'It floats.'

Umily raised her eyebrows. 'Ah. That's why you're so wet.'

'It's not perfect yet. Next time it'll be better,' said Iggy.

'Next time?' said Umily with a grin.

'Why not? We're not giving up now, are we, Hubba?'

Hubba gave him a withering look. If he wanted to drown himself in the river, next time he could do it by himself.

Iggy looked back at the spot where the boater had gone down. A few twigs and leaves were floating away. *Still, great inventions don't happen overnight*, he reasoned. All the boater needed was a few adjustments—not so many holes, for one thing. Next time he would try using logs, rather than twigs. Four or five logs bound together might work. And no mud—mud was a mistake.

Umily had hung back to wait for him. 'Coming?' she said. 'You'll get cold standing there.'

They walked along the bank and began to climb uphill towards the caves. Suddenly they were shaken by a deafening noise like the sky cracking in two. At first Iggy thought it must be thunder or a woolly mammoth jumping out of a tree, but then he saw Umily staring in the direction of the mountains. High above the valley, Old Grumbly was spewing black clouds into the sky.

'Great Urk!' gasped Hubba. 'What's that?'

Iggy shook his head. 'I don't know, but I think we better get back.'

They raced up the hill. The rest of the Urks had felt the ground shake too and had come running out of their caves to see what was happening. They stood gazing up at the distant mountains in fear. The sky was full of birds and winged lizards screeching as they swooped by. Iggy found his mum and dad outside their cave, looking pale and worried.

'What is it, Dad?' he asked.

'Old Grumbly,' replied Dad. 'Her's never done this before.'

'Will we be all right?'

''Course we will,' said Mum, putting a big arm round him. 'Your uncle will know what to do.'

They looked around, searching for Chief Hammerhead, but he was nowhere to be seen. At the first thundering rumble, he had fled into his cave and hadn't come out.

Chapter 4
Looking for Nonecks

Meanwhile, many miles to the north, two weary figures were trudging through a dismal landscape of fog and bog. The fog made it impossible to see where they were going and the bogs made every step dangerous. It was all too easy to blunder into one and find yourself sinking up to your neck in oozing brown mud.

Snark couldn't imagine why anyone would want to live in this bog-ridden wilderness. There were no hills, no rivers or forests, and no caves to shelter from the clammy cold. The fog played tricks on his imagination. Just now, for instance, he'd imagined that he'd seen someone, but when he looked again there was nothing there. He leaned on his spear to rest. They'd been travelling for three days and all they'd found was this miserable swamp that gave him the collywobbles. All around were eerie sucking sounds, mud flupping and flopping as if it were alive.

'What are we doing here?' he sighed. 'Can't us go back now?'

'I told you, not till we find 'em,' snapped Borg.

'They can't live here, Dad. No one does.'

Borg peered into the swirling mist. 'Maybe,' he said, 'maybe not. Maybe them are watching us right now.'

The hairs prickled on the back of Snark's neck. He would have turned and run if he hadn't been terrified of falling into a bog. He'd never actually seen a

Noneck, except in his nightmares, but he knew that they were cruel, savage creatures, tall as giants and ten times as ugly. For a brief moment the fog cleared and he caught his breath.

'Dad,' he said in a trembling voice, 'there's something there.'

'Where?'

'There!' He pointed ahead. Borg grasped his spear tightly, peering into the fog. He could see nothing but more fog.

'You're imagining things,' he muttered.

'I'm not! It were there. Let's go back, please!'

Borg shivered with the cold. He was beginning to wonder if coming to the Farlands was such a good idea after all. What if the Nonecks didn't like the sound of his plan or murdered them before he even had a chance to explain it? Still, it was a bit late to think of turning back now. He called out.

'Hello? Anyone there?'

Silence. Suddenly something hummed through the air, narrowly missing his ear. It was a spear with a jagged point. Borg decided it was never too late to admit you might have made a mistake.

'Run!' he cried. 'RUN, you fool!'

They turned and ran. Harsh shouts rang out, coming from all sides. Another spear went zipping overhead. They tore blindly through the fog, splashing through marshy puddles and slipping in the mud. Borg ducked his head trying to make himself a smaller target. He overtook Snark and leapt a big clump of reeds. Too late he saw what lay on the other side.

THLUUUUUUPPP!

He sank up to his knees in the bog. A moment later Snark landed beside him.

'AARGH! IT'S A BOG!' wailed Snark needlessly.

'I know. Get off me!'

'But Dad, I'm sinking!'

'So am I, you big lump, and you're making it worse!'

Borg looked around. Tall figures loomed out of the fog like ghosts. They stood at the edge of the bog, leaning on their spears and sticks, watching. Borg took in their flat ugly faces, stooped shoulders and impressively hairy chests. Nonecks. The one with a string of dirty yellow bones round his neck spoke or grunted something.

'Urgs!'

Borg twisted his head round. 'Please help us! We're sinking!'

Krakkk, Chief of the Noneck tribe, nodded, showing his jagged teeth.

'Yes, you stinking. HA HA HA!'

The rest of his tribe joined in the laughter as if this was the best joke they'd heard in ages—which it probably was. (Nonecks are not famous for their sense of humour.)

'Listen!' pleaded Borg desperately. 'I am Borg. This is my son. We just want to talk!'

Krakkk squatted down beside the bog. 'Talk, Urg,' he said.

'But first pull us out—or we'll die!'

The bog was swallowing them bit by bit. The thick brown sludge was up to Borg's chest and every second it sucked him in deeper. Snark grabbed him round the neck.

40

'DAD! HEEELP!'

'Not now, boy,' snapped Borg. 'Listen,' he begged Krakkk. 'I can help you. I can give you Hammerhead!'

'Hoggerhead? I never hear of him.'

'Hammerhead, Chief of the Urks. You remember? He beat you.'

Krakkk's face darkened. Last winter his tribe had captured a small boy called Iggy and forced him to lead them to the Valley of Urk. But Iggy had escaped and warned his tribe. The Urks had driven the Noneck invaders back, inflicting a humiliating defeat on them. Ever since that day Krakkk had sworn by all the gods he would be avenged.

'Krakkk great warrior,' he said. 'Kill many Urg.'

'Yes, I know,' nodded Borg. 'But I can help you beat Hammerhead for good.'

Krakkk frowned. 'Why you help? You Urg.'

'Because we want the same thing!' panted Borg. 'I want Hammerhead dead. Iggy too.'

'Iggy?' Krakkk's eyes flickered with sudden interest.

'Yes. He's the next Chief.'

41

The mud was up to Borg's neck. Snark was making strange noises like someone gargling porridge.

Krakkk stood up suddenly and barked an order to his men. They went running off and came back with a long branch. It slapped on to the bog close to Borg's head. He seized hold of it for dear life and grabbed Snark by the hair with his other hand. The Nonecks heaved and grunted, pulling them out of the slime. They emerged with a horrible sound like a snail being sucked from its shell.

SHLUUUUUUUUUUUUUUP!

The two Urks lay on the bank, limp and panting, plastered with stinking brown mud. Borg would have happily stayed there a bit longer, but rough hands dragged him in front of the Noneck Chief. Krakkk pressed an axe-blade to his throat by way of greeting.

'Speak, Urg,' he said. 'Tell me this plan. Maybe I don't keel you.'

Borg gulped. He began to talk fast, explaining the bargain he was offering. When he had finished Krakkk removed the axe from his throat and ran his finger over the blade thoughtfully.

'You help Krakkk—against tribe of Urg?'

'Yes,' nodded Borg. 'Hammerhead and Iggy are yours. Do what you want with them.'

Krakkk considered this. 'And you, Urg, what you get?'

'I become Chief—High Chief of the Urks,' said Borg, wiping mud from his eyes. 'You take any furs or flints you want, then you go.'

'Go?'

'Yes, go home—back where you came from,' said Borg.

Krakkk narrowed his eyes. For a moment Borg thought he might throw them back in the bog. But he drew back his lips, showing his horrible teeth.

'Good,' he said. 'Krakkk do this.'

Borg heaved a sigh of relief. 'Then we has a bargain,' he said.

'Bargin,' nodded Krakkk. 'Now we swear oath—in blood.'

'Ah,' said Borg, swallowing hard. He was hoping they could just shake hands.

Chapter 5
Wise Words

Back in the valley, the Urks had plenty of problems of their own. For two days and nights Old Grumbly had continued to boom and rumble, filling the sky with curtains of black smoke. Much of the time it was hard to tell if it was day or night. Bits of ash fell like snowflakes, getting in people's eyes and turning their hair to grey. The Urks were used to rain, hail and blizzards, but this was much worse. Many of them hid in their caves, covering their ears to shut out the noises echoing through the valley. Sometimes Old Grumbly was silent, but that was almost worse. Then everyone was on edge, wondering when the next explosion would come and if it would crack the sky open like an egg. The wailing women went from cave to cave moaning that they were all going to die.

On the third morning, Iggy went looking for the Chief and found him lying in the dark of his cave.

'Uncle Ham, what are you doing?' he asked.

'Nothing,' grunted the Chief, from under a pile of furs.

'Everyone's gone mad out there. They think the world's ending!'

'Maybe it is.'

'But you're the Chief,' said Iggy. 'Shouldn't you maybe do something?'

'Like what?'

'I don't know. Go out there. Say something—anything!'

The Chief's face peeped out. 'We're all going to die!' he moaned.

45

'Oh, for Urk's sake!' Iggy didn't hear Umily come in but he could tell she wasn't in a patient mood. She marched over to her father and grabbed the furs off him.

'Get up, you lazy lump!' she scolded.

'But Umily . . . Oww! Argh!' cried Hammerhead as she kicked and walloped him.

'Get up! Now! Put on your necklace!'

'What for?'

'Because you're going to do something useful,' stormed Umily.

*   *   *

A Council of the Elders was held that evening at the Standing Stone. All the Urks attended, anxious to hear how their Chief was going to save them from *The End of the World*. Iggy found himself seated at the front, beside the six white-haired elders, since Hammerhead insisted that this was where a future Chief belonged. Personally, he would have felt much more comfortable sitting next to Hubba, with the rest of the tribe. Being at the front made him

46

self-conscious—he'd only ever spoken once at a meeting of the elders and he didn't want to do it again.

Once they were settled, Hammerhead rose to his feet and addressed the tribe.

'Are us all here? Anybody not?'

One of the elders raised his hand.

'Put it down, Sedric,' sighed his neighbour.

'What about Borg?' asked someone at the back. Heads turned and there was a brief discussion. It seemed that no one had seen Borg for days—not since he had set off for the forest with his son to go hunting.

'No matter. We'll start without him,' said Hammerhead. If Borg had got himself eaten by a wild animal, that was his problem. Hammerhead surveyed the rows of faces in the firelight.

'I won't beat about the rocks,' he said. 'Things look bad, maybe badder than ever before.'

'Woe!' wailed the wailing woman.

'Silence!' roared Hammerhead. 'Urks has lived in this valley since the beginning of time. Nothing is going to drive us away, not even Old Grumbly.'

47

In the distance the volcano rumbled, almost as if it had been listening. The Urks gasped and clutched at each other. Only Gaga the Wise remained calm, sitting cross-legged among the elders nodding his head as if listening to silent music. Hammerhead waited for the whimpering to die down, then turned to the elders, asking for their counsel.

'Maybe if we put us fingers in our ears,' suggested one.

'How's that going to help?'

'What?'

'I said how's that going to help?'

'Sorry, I can't hear. I got my fingers in my ears.'

Iggy rolled his eyes. Meetings of the elders were always like this—you asked a simple question and got a dozen stupid answers. It drove him round the bend.

'We're missing the point,' he sighed loudly. A dozen heads turned in his direction. Iggy felt his cheeks burning. He hadn't meant to speak—the words had just spilled out.

'Um ... what I mean is,' he stammered, 'how do we know the world's ending?'

48

'Are you deaf?' asked someone. 'Listen to it!'

'But maybe it's just like rain,' said Iggy.

'Talk sense, boy,' grumbled Hammerhead. 'What's rain got to do with it?'

'I mean when it rains here, we don't know if it's raining in the mountains. It's the same thing—maybe the world isn't ending everywhere, just here. If we leave the valley, we might be safe.'

Hammerhead frowned. 'Leave? *Leave* the Valley of Urk?'

'We may have to,' said Iggy.

This met with howls of protest.

'We can't *leave*!'

'We'd all die!'

'We'd be eaten by wolves!'

Everyone was shouting at once. What Iggy suggested was madness, unthinkable. Urks belonged in the Valley of Urk. They'd always lived there and nothing on earth would persuade them to live anywhere else. Besides, where would they go? Most Urks had never been further than the forest. If you went too far you would fall off the edge of the world—everyone knew that.

Iggy eventually sat down, feeling that it was pointless to argue.

'Gaga the Wise, what has you to say?' asked Hammerhead, turning to the ancient elder. The crowd went quiet. Gaga was the oldest of the tribe and his opinion was always respected. For a minute he remained silent, so that Iggy wondered if he'd heard the question. Finally his eyes snapped open.

'The question is not where, it is why,' he said. 'Why are the Ancestors angry?'

Hammerhead looked baffled. He hadn't the foggiest idea.

'Perhaps we should ask them,' said Gaga, folding his hands in his lap.

The Urks murmured agreement—finally someone was talking sense. It stood to reason, if the Ancestors were angry then they must find out why.

'But no one's ever seen the Ancestors,' said Hammerhead. 'How can we ask them?'

Gaga the Wise raised a bony finger, pointing to the mountains. 'Seek them out,' he said. 'Someone must climb into the clouds and speak for the tribe.'

50

Hammerhead stared. 'Climb Old Grumbly? Won't that be dangerous?'

'Very,' nodded Gaga. 'That's why you must go.'

'*Me?*' Hammerhead's eyes widened.

'You are the High Chief. You must save your people.'

'Yes, but . . . but my knees aren't so good,' stammered Hammerhead. 'And I don't like heights.'

Gaga was unmoved. 'Take a companion,' he said. 'Someone young and strong.'

Hammerhead nodded. A companion was a good idea—that way he could send them on ahead to see if it was safe. He looked around for a volunteer but everyone seemed anxious to avoid his eye. Finally he noticed a hand raised in the air.

'IGGY!' he boomed. 'I knew you wouldn't let

me down.'

'What? No!' croaked Iggy. 'I was only—'

'Good, then that's settled,' said Hammerhead, clapping him on the back. 'We set off at dawn—unless of course the world ends before then.'

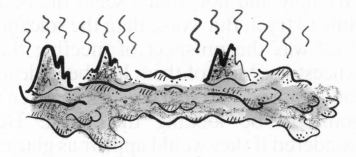

Chapter 6
All of a Lava

At first light the next morning, Iggy and Chief Hammerhead took the rough track that wound uphill in the direction of the mountains. They were joined by Umily and Hubba, who insisted on going with them at least as far as the foothills. Old Grumbly loomed in the distance, a plume of cloud curling from its mouth like smoke from a dragon's nostrils.

Iggy had never been to the High Mountains before but the closer they got the more he had a bad feeling. No one had ever climbed to the top of Old Grumbly and now didn't seem the best time to try it. But worse than the volcano itself was the prospect of meeting the Ancestors. Most of them had been dead for hundreds of years so they weren't going to be looking their best. He wondered if they would appear as ghosts or spirits, or maybe as skeletons with wormy hair.

As they climbed the foothills, they entered a strange world of swirling cloud and falling ash. Hammerhead had brought gift offerings of nuts and yumberries for the Ancestors, though typically he'd eaten half of them on the way. They paused by a stream, gazing up at the mountain in awed silence. Hubba blew out his cheeks.

'Yikes! I wouldn't like to climb that!'

Iggy gave him a look. 'Yeah, thanks, Hubba.'

Umily looked at her father. 'We could go back. It's not too late.'

Hammerhead shook his head. The future of the tribe was in their hands. Besides, he didn't want people calling him a wimp.

'Wish us luck,' he said.

'Best of luck,' said Hubba. 'Say hello to the Ancestors for me.'

'We'll be waiting right here for you,' said Umily. She hugged her father one more time and gave Iggy a grateful smile. Then the two of them began climbing up the steep rocky slope.

For the first hour they made good progress, but as they climbed higher the landscape grew stranger and more barren. The earth was dry and cracked with a powdery grey crust. Here and there grew stumpy black trees that looked like giants' fists bursting through the ground. Nothing crawled or crept or made a sound apart from the weird groans and rumbles of the mountain which seemed to come from under their feet. Now and then Iggy would jump back in alarm as a jet of steam hissed up through a crack in the ground. And all the time the air grew warmer and heavier as they drew closer to the volcano's rim.

55

Iggy halted and wiped the sweat from his brow as he waited for the Chief to catch up. Hammerhead's face was pink as a lobster and bits of ash were caught in his hair and beard. If he was ever going to reach the top Iggy thought he might need carrying.

'Got to . . . rest,' he panted, flopping down on a rock.

'Not far now,' coaxed Iggy.

'I've gone all dizzy,' Hammerhead moaned. 'Maybe you should go on without me.'

'I think it's safer if we stick together,' said Iggy. There was no way he was facing the Spirits of the Ancestors on his own. Old Grumbly rumbled loudly as if growing impatient. Hammerhead got to his feet.

'Scared?' he asked.

'No,' said Iggy. 'Well, maybe a bit.'

Hammerhead grinned. 'Me too. Still, what's the worst that can happen, eh?'

We could die a horrible death, thought Iggy, but it was probably bad luck to say it.

They started the final climb towards

the top. This high up there were no trees or boulders, only a desert of grey dunes and valleys. The ground grew hotter as they climbed so that it burned the soles of Iggy's feet. Hammerhead went on tiptoe, making little 'Ohh ahh eee!' sounds with every step. Above them the ground seemed to rise to a peak where the smoke was billowing out. It was strangely beautiful, in a terrifying sort of way. Iggy didn't think the heat would allow them much closer, but there was no sign of the Ancestors.

'You got the offerings?' he asked.

Hammerhead felt in his furs and produced a purple mess of berries.

'That's it?' said Iggy.

'I were hungry!'

'Go on then—you better speak to them.'

'Right.' Hammerhead hung back. 'What shall I say?'

'I don't know! It wasn't my idea.'

Hammerhead blew out his cheeks. 'You do it,' he said, offering the berries.

'What? You're the Chief!'

'But you're younger. You can run faster. Please.'

Iggy sighed heavily. He might have known this would happen. He took the squashed berries from Hammerhead and crept up the slope towards the smoking crater.

'Hello? Anyone there?'

No answer.

Iggy glanced back at Hammerhead, who looked ready to leg it at any moment.

He took a deep breath and called out: 'I seek an audience with the Spirits of the Ancestors—if they've got a minute.'

BLOOB! BLOB! BLUB!

Iggy peered through the smoke to see where the strange noise was coming from. The volcano had a mouth—wider than the mouth of a cave—and from this the smoke was belching into the sky. But that wasn't what made Iggy's stomach flip over. Inside the mouth he glimpsed

58

something red that bubbled and heaved like boiling stew.

BOOOOOOOM!

Iggy dropped the squashed berries and fled. Hammerhead was ahead of him, moving surprisingly fast for someone with bad knees. They tore down the mountain—over the scorching ash, past the hissing blowholes, jumping over boulders and sending pebbles racing down the slope. They didn't stop until they reached the lower slopes where the stumpy trees grew. It took a full minute before either of them could speak.

'Well?' panted Hammerhead. 'You saw 'em?'

'Who?'

'The Ancestors, you fool! Did they answer?'

Iggy shook his head. 'No. There was no one there—just a hole like a giant mouth. But I saw inside . . .'

'And?' said Hammerhead. 'It were full of spiders?'

'No,' said Iggy. 'It's like a fire—a sea of fire, burning and bubbling.'

Hammerhead looked disappointed.

He'd been hoping for spiders at least.

'That were all?'

'All?' said Iggy. 'Don't you see? All this smoke and ash, it comes from down there, in the mountain's belly. Any time now it could erupt!'

'How do you mean?'

'Erupt! Explode!' said Iggy, waving his hands. 'And if it does, the fire will overflow. It'll sweep down and reach the valley!'

'Crumbs,' said Hammerhead.

'We'll be wiped out!' said Iggy. 'All of us. Burned to a frazzle!'

'Not if we stay in our caves.'

'It won't make any difference. You can't run or hide—not from this.'

'Then what can us do?'

'Leave,' replied Iggy. 'While there's still time. We've got to get away from here.'

Hammerhead nodded sadly. Iggy was probably right though none of this was going to be easy to explain. Rivers of fire, bellies and eruptings—it might be better to say they'd chatted to the Ancestors who had suggested they all take a short holiday.

60

those men didn't look like their tribe. They were bigger and uglier, moving as if they were in a hurry.

*   *   *

At the foot of the slope Hubba and Umily were waiting for them anxiously. They'd heard the mountain rumble and had feared the worst. Iggy explained what he'd seen inside the crater and the terrible danger they were all in. They hurried back towards the Valley of Urk, knowing there was no time to lose.

As they came over the hill, Umily stopped in her tracks.

'Look! What's that?' She pointed to the valley below.

'The river. It's that green thing,' answered Hubba.

'No, not that, *that*!' Umily was pointing to the bend in the river upstream. Iggy caught sight of a line of dark figures moving swiftly along the bank under the trees. They were heading towards the crossing point further down.

'Hunting   party?'   suggested Hammerhead.

Iggy shook his head. Urks didn't hunt in such large numbers and in any case these men didn't look like their tribe. They were bigger and uglier, moving as if they were in a hurry.

'They're not Urks,' he said. 'They're Nonecks.'

Chapter 7

The Wrath of Krakkk

Crouched among the trees by the river, Borg made sure he kept out of sight. No one seemed to have spotted their approach. Up the hill he could see a few Urks moving around outside the caves. The only noise disturbing the peace was the occasional low rumble from the mountains. Borg thought this was a little strange—he'd never known the mountains to have bellyache before. Still, he had far more important things to consider. He had waited a long time to be rid of Hammerhead and now, with Krakkk's help, he would finally become Chief. It was lucky that the Noneck was as dim as a dung beetle or he might have decided to claim the valley for himself.

'Let me and Snark go ahead,' said Borg. 'I don't want it to look like we

63

come together.'

Krakkk frowned. 'Why not want?'

'They mustn't know I has anything to do with this. Remember what we agreed?'

Krakkk nodded impatiently. 'The boy and the fat one are mine.'

'Hammerhead. You can't miss him—he's hairy as a grizzler,' said Borg. 'Remember, once they surrender, you and me pretend to quarrel.'

'Quirrel?' said Krakkk.

'Quarrel. Fight.'

'Ah, fight,' said Krakkk with a smile. 'I keel you good.'

'No! No killing,' said Borg. 'We been over this a hundred times. We argue—then you leave. Run away.'

Krakkk scowled. 'You think Krakkk is scaredy-clot?'

'That's what we agreed, for Urk's sake! You get Hammerhead, I become Chief. Then you take what you want and go. Got it?'

Krakkk grunted. He didn't like the way this ugly Urk talked to him, as if he was seven kinds of stupid. But there would be time for him later. First he would crush his enemies and have his revenge.

*   *   *

Up the hill, the Urks were going about their daily tasks with no idea that they were being watched. Iggy's dad picked up a pile of skins that were spotted with ash and carried them down to the river to wash. Halfway down the hill, he stopped to watch a group of young Urks playing Head-banger. It was a simple game involving two blindfolded teams charging at each other and cracking heads. The winner of the game was the last man standing (or semi-conscious). Already two of the Urks were flat on their backs moaning and clutching their heads. A third had missed everyone and was wandering around blindly, bumping into trees.

Dad smiled at the young Urks having fun and continued on his way. The river was still high after the rains and the current was strong. He waded in up to his knees and dunked the skins in the water, rubbing them clean. It was peaceful here, he thought. Nothing but the birds singing, the breeze blowing and the fish talking in low voices. *Wait a minute—fish didn't usually do that!* He looked up and locked eyes with someone hiding in the reeds. The stranger had a flat ugly face, full lips and an animal skull on his head. Dad stiffened with fear. Now he looked again, there were more of them—fifty or a hundred, crouched in the reeds and among the trees, staring right at him. *Nonecks!* He dropped the wet skins and splashed towards the bank, his heart racing. As he climbed out something thudded into the muddy bank. A hunting axe. He tore up the hill, flattening one of the blindfolded Urks who got in his way.

'SOUND THE HORN! WE'RE UNDER ATTACK!'

*   *   *

Many are the stories told and the songs

sung about the glorious victories of the Urks in battle. Unfortunately this wasn't one of them. The fighting was over in roughly ten minutes. Taken by surprise, the Urks were utterly defeated. By the end, five had been wounded and around a hundred taken prisoner. One of the Nonecks meanwhile had suffered a slightly grazed knee when he slipped in a puddle.

Krakkk had his enemies rounded up and stripped of their weapons. He stood on a rock, watching as they were herded together.

'You my slaves,' he gloated. 'Now you bow to Krakkk.'

He scanned the dirty faces, searching for one in particular.

'Where is fat one? Chief of Urg?' he demanded.

'Not here,' came the reply.

Krakkk glared at them. 'Do not tell flibs.'

'It's true.' Iggy's dad pushed his way to the front. 'Hammerhead's not here,' he said. 'But he'll be back—with a proper big army.'

Krakkk laughed, shaking his head in

pity. 'You Urgs, always the big clevers, hmm? But Krakkk not the stupid. You are the stupids now.'

He turned to his men and growled something in his own language. Two of the Nonecks stepped forward and jabbed at the prisoners with their spears, forcing them to move. They hadn't gone far when there was a scuffle in the crowd and one broke free. It was Borg.

'Hey, Krakkk!' he shouted.

The Noneck Chief turned round slowly to face him. Borg marched right up to

him, till they were face to face.

'Listen, you bug-ugly Noneck,' he said. 'I has had a bellyful of you.'

Krakkk stared at him coldly, his eyes wide.

'Why don't you take your flat-faced friends and crawl back to the swamp?' said Borg, actually poking him in the chest.

The silence hung in the air like a bad smell. The Urks wondered if Borg had taken leave of his senses. Krakkk's face had gone red and purple veins were

standing out on his forehead. He was swelling up like a bullfrog. Suddenly his right hand shot out and clamped round Borg's neck, lifting him right off the ground.

'UGLY?' he seethed. 'You call Krakkk UGLY? I KEEEL YOU!'

Borg was struggling to breathe. 'No, listen!' he croaked. 'Remember what we . . . ?'

'STRUGA!' bellowed Krakkk, tossing Borg through the air like a rag doll. He spat out an order to his men. One of them dragged Borg to his feet and pushed him back into the scrum of prisoners. The Urks were herded at spear-point to the edge of a deep hole known as the Snake Pit. The good news was that there were no snakes in it right now. The bad news was that that left more room for them. Borg was pushed in first, followed by the rest, most of whom landed on top of him.

'OUCH!'
'OOOF!
'Mind my . . . YARGH!'

Chapter 8

Things Can Only Get Wetter

While this was happening down in the valley, Iggy and his friends had watched events unfold from high on the hill. The sky had grown darker.

'Shouldn't us do something?' asked Hubba.

'Such as?'

'Well, you know—attack.'

'Attack?' said Iggy. 'With four of us?'

'We could spread out,' suggested Hubba.

Iggy gave him a weary look.

'Never mind, things could be worse,' said Hammerhead cheerfully.

'Really?' said Iggy. 'They've stolen our caves, captured our whole tribe and—oh yes—the world might end any moment. How can it be any worse?'

'At least it's not raining,' said Hammerhead.

There was a rumble of thunder. Heavy raindrops began to plop from the sky.

'Oh,' said Hammerhead.

The rain warmed to its task, pouring down as if the Ancestors were emptying their bathwater. It dripped off branches and bounced off stones. Iggy hugged himself, shivering with cold, and watched the river swell higher. It reminded him that there was still one ray of hope.

'The boater!' he said. 'We could use that!'

Hubba groaned.

'I thought her sunk,' said Umily.

'It did, but I've been working on a better one made of logs. This one will float.'

'What's a boater?' asked Hammerhead, who was looking confused.

'It's like sticks,' Iggy explained. 'Sticks float, right? So does this.'

'Except when it sinks,' said Hubba.

'It won't sink!' scowled Iggy. 'We can use it to escape.'

'How?' asked Hammerhead. 'They'd see us.'

'Not if we wait until dark,' said Iggy.

'But what about the others?' Umily objected. 'They're prisoners. We can't just leave 'em.'

Iggy had forgotten that. His mum and dad were trapped in the snakepit, along with the rest of the tribe. 'We'll just have to take them with us,' he said.

No one answered. Iggy had come up with some wild ideas in the past but this was probably the looniest yet. There were a hundred Urks and he wanted to rescue them by floating them downriver on some sort of log. In Hubba's opinion they might as well jump off a cliff and have done with it.

*   *   *

Down in the snakepit, things were beginning to look desperate. The Urks were trying not to panic. For one thing they were squashed together like beans in a tin, but worse still, the pit was filling up fast. When the rain had started there was only a puddle lapping around their ankles. Now the water was up to their waists and still rising. They had tried yelling out for help but the Nonecks couldn't hear (mainly because they had retired to the caves to keep out of the rain).

'Dad,' shivered Snark, 'I'm coooold!'

'Stop whining!' snapped Borg. 'We're all cold.'

'But what if no one comes?'

'They will!'

'But what if they don't, Dad? We'll drown! We'll all die!'

'You'll die if you don't stop moaning!' said Borg.

The rain was bouncing off the water and running in rivers down the sides of the pit. Even when Snark had tried to climb out, treading on people's heads, he couldn't reach the top and slithered back where he started.

A flash of light lit up the heavens followed by a deafening rumble.

'What were that?' asked Snark, clutching his dad's arm.

'Old Grumbly,' answered Borg.

They turned their heads towards the mountain where the sky was an angry red. Something strange was happening.

'Woe! For the end is upon us!' wailed an old woman.

'Put a rock in it!' thundered Borg. 'Listen! You hear that?'

They fell silent, clinging to each other in fear. There was a different sound in the darkness: hushed whispers and feet splashing through puddles. Suddenly they jumped back as a huge, hairy face loomed above them.

'Hammy!' cried Iggy's dad. 'We thought you was dead! Where's Iggy?'

'Here!' Iggy's face came into view, along with Hubba and Umily. The Urks in the pit surged forward. They cried out, begging to be saved.

'Quiet! They'll hear you!' hissed Iggy.

'Iggy's right,' boomed the Chief.

'Everyone stay calm and we'll get you out.'

Umily brought a rope made of knotted creepers, which was lowered down into the pit. Hammerhead and Hubba held tightly to one end, providing an anchor, while the Urks clambered up. They emerged one at a time looking like drowned rats and huddled in the rain, waiting for the others to join them. It took for ever. Iggy noticed the rain was starting to ease. Dawn wasn't far off. At any moment the Nonecks might emerge from the caves and see them. He staggered as Old Grumbly made the ground shake again.

At last there were only two Urks left in the pit—Borg and Snark. Umily began to lower the rope again, but Iggy's dad stopped her.

'Wait,' he said. 'How does we know this weren't their fault?'

'What?' said Borg. 'Don't be stupid!'

'Think about it. Where's Borg been all this time?' asked Dad.

'Hunting!' snapped Borg. 'I been hunting with Snark.'

'And the hour he comes back we're

attacked by Nonecks. Don't that strike you as funny?'

Hammerhead nodded. 'Hmm. If you put it like that.'

'The rope—hurry up!' pleaded Borg.

'I'm drowning!' moaned Snark.

Iggy glanced at the sky, which was growing lighter in the east. 'We need to hurry,' he urged. 'Do we take them or not, Chief?'

Hammerhead looked down at the two muddy faces. He had never trusted Borg.

'Leave 'em,' he said.

Snark started wailing like a baby.

'NO! Get me out! It were his idea. I never did nothing!'

'Shut up, you idiot!' growled Borg.

'They'll hear you!' hissed Iggy.

But the warning came too late. Already they could hear shouts from the caves above and swift footsteps running down the hill.

Chapter 9
Rabbit Run

The Urks blundered into each other in their haste to get away. But they needn't have bothered. The Nonecks already had them encircled, cutting off their escape. Krakkk stepped forward, carrying a smoking torch in one hand and his double-headed axe in the other. He leered at Iggy.

'Well, well, Urg boy. I knowed you

come back. I see you bring your grandpa.'

'I'm his uncle,' replied the Chief with dignity. 'Hammerhead, High Chief of the Urks.'

'High Chief?' laughed Krakkk. 'Look like fat chief to me.'

The Nonecks laughed—it was always safest to laugh if their Chief did. Another boom shook the valley and a flock of flying lizards swooped over, their wings beating the air. Iggy glanced at the mountains but Krakkk paid no attention. A little thunderstorm didn't scare him.

'So, Urg,' he said, coming close to Hammerhead. 'Shall I keel you now?'

'Actually I'm a bit busy,' said Hammerhead. 'How about tomorrow?'

Krakkk spat on the ground in disgust. 'You Urgs! Always the big scaredy clots.'

'Who is?' bristled Hammerhead. 'Give me an axe, then we'll see who's scared.'

Krakkk looked at him, twirling the axe in his hand. He could slay this miserable Urk by chopping off his fat head, but that would be too easy. Why not have some sport instead?

'Krakkk is fair,' he said. 'You want

to live? I give you chance for save your skins.'

He pointed down the slope. 'Run to the forest,' he said. 'Run like rabbit.'

Hammerhead looked uneasy. There had to be some catch—Krakkk wasn't going to let them get away as easily as that. Maybe he had some kind of game in mind? He hoped it didn't involve counting because he was rubbish at that.

They didn't have to wait long to find out. At an order from their Chief, a dozen Noneck warriors spread themselves across the hill. They had spears at the ready and one or two of them bent down to pick up hefty rocks. Iggy felt his legs turn to jelly. This was a rabbit hunt and they were the rabbits. The moment they set off down the hill the Nonecks would pick them off with their spears. Judging from their grinning faces, they were confident no one would escape. They were skilled hunters used to hitting a deer at fifty paces. Even if they ran like the wind, Iggy knew their chances of reaching the forest alive were slim.

'We ready,' smiled Krakkk. 'Who want to go first?'

No one spoke. The only sound was a thin wailing voice begging for help. Iggy realised they had forgotten all about Snark, who was still trapped in the snakepit with his dad.

Krakkk turned his head. 'Fetch them,' he ordered.

The two Urks were dragged from the muddy pit. Borg was led to the top of the hill where he stood shivering and scared out of his wits. He knew something bad was about to happen but he couldn't work out what. He gazed at the line of tall Noneck warriors waiting with their spears.

'I count to three. Then you run,' said Krakkk.

'Run where?'

'To forest. If you reach, you live. If not, you die.'

'But wait!' gasped Borg. 'They got spears—they'll kill me!'

'One,' counted Krakkk. 'Two . . .'

'Run, Dad!' cried Snark.

Borg didn't wait for three, hurling himself down the slope as if he were being chased by a swarm of bees. He made straight for the river, knowing his

81

only chance was to get across and reach the cover of the trees. Mud splattered his legs and his arms whirled as he slipped and slid, trying to stay on his feet. The Noneck warriors let him get halfway down the hill, just to make things more interesting. Then they drew back their arms and hurled their spears. One landed to Borg's left and another just short of him. The rock that followed was more accurate. It struck Borg square on the head. He kept running for a few paces before falling flat. He didn't get up. Iggy couldn't tell if he was dead or nursing the mother of all headaches. The Nonecks cheered anyway—so far they'd scored full points.

Krakkk grunted with satisfaction. He turned back to the other Urks, who were beginning to wish they'd stayed in the snakepit.

'You!' he said, pointing to Hammerhead. 'And you, Urg boy.'

This was directed at Iggy. He looked at Hubba, who gave him a thumbs up. Umily hugged her father tightly, squashing her nose against his hairy chest. Krakkk pulled them apart and shoved the Chief towards the top of the hill. In a daze, Iggy took his place beside him. He glanced back at his parents, who were watching helplessly. *This is probably the last time I'll see them or this old valley*, thought Iggy. It was a pity it was drizzling with rain. In the distance Old Grumbly was still rumbling as if working itself into a rage.

Hammerhead leaned closer, lowering his voice.

'So. Got any cunning plans?' he asked.

'Run like crazy,' replied Iggy.

Hammerhead nodded. 'You would have made a good Chief, Iggy,' he said.

'You too,' said Iggy. 'I mean . . . you are.'

'Am I?'

'Everyone says so. Well, nearly everyone.'

Krakkk wanted to get on with it. He started to count.

'One . . .'

Iggy crouched forward, head down, fists bunched, ready to run for his life. It was just like a game of Boulderball, he told himself, except that in this case the other team were armed with

83

spears. A raindrop was hanging from Hammerhead's nose.

'Two . . . three!'

They burst down the hill. Iggy slalomed from side to side, hoping to present a more difficult target. He had already left Hammerhead way behind, but there was no helping that. The river below looked impossibly far away. Even if by some miracle they reached it, they wouldn't be safe till they made it across, into the trees. Iggy pounded through the mud, his feet flying. He heard the first spear zip past his left shoulder and wheeled away sharply to the right. He was running flat out but the spears were coming fast, falling like rain. Ahead the ground fell away suddenly—the slope was too steep and he didn't see the muddy puddle till he hit it. Suddenly his feet slid from under him and he was tumbling head over heels down the hill. He rolled to a stop, muddy and winded, just before something heavy slammed into him— Hammerhead. Iggy panicked, struggling to get up. Lying in the mud they were an easy target for the Noneck marksmen. Any moment now a spear might . . .

KABOOOOOM!

The whole world rocked as if a giant had reached down and shaken it like a ball. Iggy thought for the moment he

had gone deaf. Staggering to his feet, he heard shrieks and cries from up the hill. The Nonecks had forgotten them and were staring in terror at the mountains. It had finally happened. Old Grumbly had erupted! Giant red-black clouds mushroomed into the sky. The mountain seemed to be melting—or at least something strange was happening. Waves of red-hot lava were pouring from the crater and running down the sides.

'Thundering   Urk!'   gasped Hammerhead. 'The world is ending!'

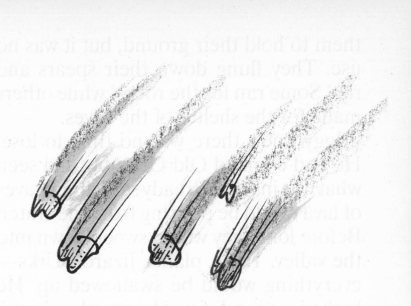

Chapter 10

Sink or Swim

The Nonecks had never seen an erupting volcano before but they were pretty sure it wasn't safe. With each boom the red fire leapt into the air and the valley shook again. The gods were angry—in fact judging by the noise, they were furious.

'Hella bella! Scarpa!' yelled the terrified Nonecks. Krakkk tried to force them to hold their ground, but it was no use. They flung down their spears and ran. Some ran for the rocks, while others made for the shelter of the caves.

Iggy knew there was no time to lose. He had climbed Old Grumbly and seen what was inside. Already scorching waves of lava would be pouring from the crater. Before long they would sweep down into the valley. Trees, plants, lizards, Urks— everything would be swallowed up. He looked around for Hammerhead and grabbed his arm.

'Quick, get everyone to the river!' he yelled above the din.

Hammerhead gaped at him. 'The river? But I can't swim!'

'Never mind that, just do it!' shouted Iggy.

It was too late to run away. They needed to get out of here fast and Iggy could think of only one way. Whether or not it would work was another matter.

The Urks were running down towards them, dragging crying children along. Iggy stood with his arms raised, shouting at them to gather at the river. He caught sight of Umily and Hubba and told them to spread the word.

'Wait for me by the crossing,' he panted.

'Why? Where you going?' asked Hubba.

'No time to explain!' shouted Iggy as he ran off, ducking under the trees, and disappeared from sight. Hammerhead, Hubba and Umily did their best to round everyone up and calm the panic, though the thundering booms from Old Grumbly didn't help much. Moments later they caught sight of Iggy. He was coming down the river, paddling some sort of wooden craft with a stick twice his size. It was a raft made of a dozen logs lashed together.

'You got to be joking!' groaned Hubba.

Iggy jumped into the water and began pulling the raft towards the bank.

'Get them on! Quick!' he urged. The current was moving fast and it took all his strength to prevent the raft from being carried away.

'It'll sink! You'll drown us all!' shouted Umily.

'No, it's safe! Get on!' Iggy yelled back. Clinging to a bit of wood wasn't

Umily's idea of safe, but then neither was running from waves of fire. The Urks were huddled on the bank, too terrified to move.

'Come on!' cried Iggy impatiently. 'Chief, you tell them.'

Hammerhead made up his mind. He was too out of breath to run any further so he might as well take his chances with drowning. He waded into the water, yelling at the Urks to follow. Another boom from Old Grumbly persuaded them he might be right. They plunged in, splashing towards the raft. There wasn't enough room for everyone, but they crowded on anyhow, piling on top of each other while the raft dipped lower in the water. Many of the men had to cling to the sides, hoping for the best. Iggy looked for the last time at the valley and the angry volcano, then pushed off with his stick. In seconds the raft was borne away on the strong current at alarming speed. The Urks howled and clung to each other in fright as the raft tipped, spun and scraped against rocks. Chief Hammerhead was curled in a ball with his eyes shut, praying that the gods would take him quickly. Past Giant's Rock the crowded raft swept downstream and turned the corner, leaving the Valley of Urk far behind.

Chapter 11

The High Life

Morning came and the raft was drifting slowly in a quiet stretch of the river. Iggy groaned. His body ached all over. He had no idea how many miles they'd travelled or how they'd survived being tossed and spun around like a twig in a whirlpool. By some miracle they were all alive, though it was true that most of them looked sick as dogs. He struggled out from the tangled heap of bodies and looked around. The Valley of Urk was nowhere to be seen. The only trace of it was a column of grey smoke in the far north, coming from Old Grumbly.

Iggy guided the raft towards the bank with his stick. The other Urks were rousing themselves with weary groans, grumbling at those on top of them. In twos and threes they slipped off the raft and waded to the bank, where they stood blinking in the weak sunshine.

'Where on Urk are we?' asked Hubba.

'I don't know,' said Iggy. 'But wherever it is, at least the world hasn't ended.'

'How do you know?'

'Look around you. This isn't so bad. We could stay here.'

Hammerhead was wringing dirty water from his furs.

'We're Urks,' he grunted. 'We live in the Valley of Urk. We'll go back as soon as I can work out where we are.'

'Look!' Hubba's cry made them all turn. He was pointing along the river to where the bank jutted out, creating a shallow pool. It was clogged with debris from the volcano that had been swept downstream during the night. There were burnt lumps of wood, dirty bones, broken branches and even an animal skull that had once sat on the head of a Noneck warrior. But that wasn't what had caught Hubba's attention. A tree trunk floated in the shallows and slumped on top, half in the water, was a person. Hubba and Iggy waded into the river and dragged the soggy creature to the bank. When they laid him down, he spluttered, coughed and opened his eyes.

93

'Snark!' said Iggy, recognising the big ugly nose.

'Run! Run!' croaked Snark, gripping his arm and trying to escape.

'Snark, it's me,' said Iggy. 'You're safe now.'

The Urks crowded round, staring at the newcomer as if he'd landed from outer space. Snark was certainly a strange sight. His face was black with smoke. His hair stood on end and was singed down the middle, so that he resembled a startled badger. His furs were torn and ragged, with a large rip at the back leaving his bottom open to the wind. He sat up, looking at them wildly. Hammerhead came over and crouched in front of him.

'Snark, what happened? Where's Borg?' he asked.

'Gone,' croaked Snark.

'And the others? The Nonecks?'

Snark shook his head. He hadn't seen them in the fire but they couldn't have escaped.

'What about the valley? The caves?' asked Hammerhead. 'There must be something left.'

Snark stared at him dumbly. 'Gone. All gone,' he moaned. 'Everything burned.'

Iggy thought he could imagine what would have happened. Waves of scorching red lava sweeping down the hill into the valley, burning everything in their path. It was a miracle that Snark had escaped.

Hammerhead was swaying slightly, trying to take it in. The caves, the Standing Stone, his prize flint collection—all gone, wiped out in a matter of seconds. It made his head spin. How was the tribe going to survive now? Where would they go? And more importantly, would he have to go without supper?

The Urks stood speechless, none of them knowing what to say. They couldn't go back. There was no valley to go back to. They were homeless, rootless, Urkless. It was Iggy who eventually broke the stunned silence.

'It might be all right,' he said, looking about him. 'It's got the river. And there's probably a forest somewhere.'

Hammerhead stared at him. 'What are you yammering about?'

'Here,' said Iggy. 'We could live here.'

'How? There's no hill.'

'That's good,' said Iggy. 'We won't have to trog up and down it every day.'

'And what about caves?' demanded Mum. 'Where we all gonna sleep?'

Iggy hadn't thought of that. Dry, roomy caves wouldn't be so easy to find—especially ones that didn't contain bears. There were no mountains or rocky hills here, only wild grass, bushes and trees with branches reaching up to the sky. *If we were a flock of birds*, he thought, *this place would be perfect.* He put his head on one side, the way he did when he was having an idea.

'Hubba,' he said, 'help me drag that boater from the water.'

It took six of them and a lot of grunting to drag the raft up the bank and over to the foot of one of the trees. It was even harder (and took more grumbling and cursing) to haul it halfway up the tree and wedge it between two thick branches. Finally it was in position, forming a wooden platform high above the ground.

'Well?' said Iggy, perched on the high deck. 'What do you think?'

Hammerhead and the others squinted up at him from below.

'What the Urk's it meant to be?' asked the Chief.

'Isn't it obvious?'

'Not to me,' frowned Hammerhead.

Iggy grinned, spreading his hands wide.

'It's our new home!'

'Home?' said his dad. 'It's a tree!'

'Yes. Exactly!'

'We're not flamin' monkeys, boy. We live in caves.'

'But this is much better,' said Iggy. 'It's perfect, don't you see? It's got a floor and we can make a sort of roof thing to keep off the rain.'

Dad shook his head. 'Talk sense, boy. You can't live in a tree!'

'Why not?'

'Well . . . you'd fall off.'

'No you wouldn't,' said Iggy.

'Anyhow, there's no room,' argued Mum.

'There's plenty,' said Iggy. 'Come up here and see!'

They took a great deal of persuading, but finally Mum and Dad clambered up to join him. They were followed by Hubba and Umily, who were used to climbing trees, and Chief Hammerhead, who wasn't and needed a bunk-up from three of his men.

They huddled on the platform, glancing nervously at the ground below. Hammerhead was feeling rather dizzy and out of breath.

'It's amazing!' said Iggy. 'You can see for miles! Look, there's a forest over there where we can go hunting.'

Dad looked up. 'There's too much sky,' he grumbled.

But Mum was beginning to warm to the idea. 'It *is* dry,' she said. 'And there's not so much dirt as a cave.'

Dad scowled. 'Nothing wrong with a bit of dirt.'

'And we could hang skins up here to dry,' said Mum, pointing to the branches.

'We'd be safe from bears and wolves,' said Iggy. 'And at night we'd look up and see the stars!'

'Deadly!' said Hubba.

'What do you think, Hammy?' asked Dad.

They all turned to the Chief, who had

just found the courage to stand up. If you kept hold of the branches and didn't look down, it wasn't so bad. He looked at the others.

'The boy's been right before,' he said. 'He'll make a good Chief.'

'And we've got to live somewhere,' agreed Mum. 'This'll be a new start.'

'But what about the others, Iggy?' asked Hammerhead. 'We can't all squash on here.'

'That's no problem—we can build more,' said Iggy excitedly. 'There's plenty of trees to go round. We'll build enough for everyone and call them . . . um . . .'

'TREE CAVES!' cried Hubba.

'Yes, tree caves!' laughed Iggy.

It was a brilliant idea. Who could tell, one day maybe everyone would live like this!